Little Bo-Peep's Missing Sheep

D0709696

Written by Alan Durant
Illustrated by Leah-Ellen Heming

WAYLAND

Northamptonshire Libraries
& Information Service

60 000 055 130

Peters	25-May-2010
CF	£3.99

One snowy winter's morning Little Bo-Peep looked out of her window – and got a big shock. Her sheep had gone!

She picked up her crook and ran out into the meadow. No sheep! Where could they be? And where was her friend Little Boy Blue, who was supposed to be looking after them?

"Sheep, sheep!" she called.
"Little Boy Blue, where are you?"
Little Bo-Peep was puzzled.

Then she saw hoof prints in the snow. "They'll lead me to my sheep," she thought, and off she went following them.

Little Bo-Peep hadn't gone very far when she met Mary. "Have you seen my sheep?" asked Little Bo-Peep.

Mary shook her head. "Have you seen my little lamb?" she asked. "He was following me to school and, when I looked around, he'd gone. What am I going to do?" she wailed.

Mary started to cry.
"There, there," soothed Bo-Peep.
"We'll find him. He's probably with my sheep. Come with me."

So Little Bo-Peep and Mary followed the trail of hoof prints through the snow.

They went round... and round a mulberry bush, but there was no sign of any sheep, just children pretending to wash their hands.

"Have you seen my sheep?"
asked Little Bo-Peep.
"And my lamb?" added Mary.

"No," said the children, "but this is the way we go to school, go to school, go to school," they sang. And off they went.

Little Bo-Peep and Mary carried on following the hoof prints through the snow, until they came to the house that Jack built.

Little Bo-Peep knocked. "Yes?" asked Jack.

"I've lost my sheep," said Little Bo-Peep.
"And I've lost my lamb," added Mary.
"Have you seen them?" they asked.

"Come in and have a look," said Jack.
"It's my wedding party, you know."

It was very crowded in Jack's house. There was a farmer with a bag of corn, a crowing cock, a priest all shaven and shorn, a maiden all forlorn, a cow with a crumpled horn, and a dog and a cat chasing a rat.

But no sheep. But there, at the back door, were the hoof prints again!

The hoof prints led to Mary's garden. "Oh, dear," said Little Bo-Peep. Mary's garden was in a terrible state. There were silver bells and cockle shells all over the place.

"Look at my little maids," sighed Mary. "I planted them all in a row. What a mess they're in!"

At that moment they heard a noise. Snip, snip, snip. It was coming from behind the garden wall.

Snip, snip, snip.

Little Bo-Peep and Mary went to investigate.
"Oh, no!" they cried.

There was Tom, the piper's son, snipping the woolly coat of a sheep with a pair of scissors!

"Stop, thief!" Little Bo-Peep commanded. "What are you doing to my sheep?"
"I'm filling up these three bags with wool," said Tom. "One for the master and one for the dame, and one for the little boy who lives down the lane."

He grinned. "That's me!"

"But you can't do that," wailed Little Bo-Peep. "Those sheep belong to me." "And that little lamb belongs to me!" added Mary.

Tom stuck out his tongue. "Prove it!" he taunted.

Little Bo-Peep and Mary looked at each other. How could they prove the sheep and the lamb belonged to them?

Suddenly... TAN-TARAN-TARA!
It was Little Boy Blue. He'd just woken up from his sleep under a haystack and he was blowing his horn!

At once the sheep turned and ran for home. The little lamb leapt up into Mary's arms.

"I think that proves it," said Little Bo-Peep.

"Bother," said Tom with a scowl. "I'd have got a good price for those sheep at market."

"Excuse me," squealed a little voice. "Did you say market?" It was a small pig. "I'm on my way there you see, but I'm rather lost."

Tom's scowl turned to a grin once more. "I'll take you," he laughed, and he picked up the pig and away he ran!

"That naughty boy," tutted
Little Bo-Peep.
"At least you got your sheep
back," said Mary.

"And you got your little lamb,"
said Little Bo-Peep.
"Baa," bleated the little lamb happily.

Then they followed the sheep home...
bringing this tale behind them!

START READING is a series of highly enjoyable books for beginner readers. **The books have been carefully graded to match the Book Bands widely used in schools.** This enables readers to be sure they choose books that match their own reading ability.

Look out for the Band colour on the book in our Start Reading logo.

The Bands are:

Pink Band 1

Red Band 2

Yellow Band 3

Blue Band 4

Green Band 5

Orange Band 6

Turquoise Band 7

Purple Band 8

Gold Band 9

START READING books can be read independently or shared with an adult. They promote the enjoyment of reading through satisfying stories supported by fun illustrations.

Alan Durant has written many stories and poems for children of all ages. He loves nursery rhymes and often makes up his own like this one:
There was a boy called Louis-Loo / Who took his mummy to the zoo.
A lion ate her with one bite / And said, "Thank you, Louis-Loo. Goodnight."

Leah-Ellen Heming once brought back a mouse from her studio in her backpack and cycled it all the way up a very steep hill to her house, where it escaped. The mouse then had a big family, but Leah caught them all and unleashed the mice in her friend's allotment, where they now live happily ever after.